JUN 1 6

Guess What

Published in the United States of America by
Cherry Lake Publishing
Ann Arbor, Michigan
www.cherrylakepublishing.com

Content Adviser: Susan Heinrichs Gray
Reading Adviser: Marla Conn, ReadAbility, Inc.
Book Designer: Felicia Macheske

Photo Credits: © Le Do/Shutterstock Images, cover, 21; © Eric Isselee/Shutterstock Images, 10, back cover; © Olga Bogatyrenko/Shutterstock Images, 1, 15; © Yuri Kravchenko/Shutterstock Images, 3; © Jakub Zak/Shutterstock Images, 4; © Iurochkin Alexandr/Shutterstock Images, 7; © Peter Leahy/Shutterstock Images, 9; © hxdbzxy/Shutterstock Images, 12; © Tyler Fox/Shutterstock Images, 17; © kingfisher/Shutterstock Images, 18; © Andrey_Kuzmin/Shutterstock Images, back cover

Library of Congress Cataloging-in-Publication Data

Macheske, Felicia, author.
 Bright and beautiful : butterfly / Felicia Macheske.
 pages cm. — (Guess what)
 Summary: "Guess What: Bright and Beautiful: Butterfly provides young curious readers with striking visual clues and simply written hints. Using the photos and text, readers rely on visual literacy skills, reading, and reasoning as they solve the insect mystery. Clearly written facts give readers a deeper understanding of how the butterfly lives. Additional text features, including a glossary and an index, help students locate information and learn new words"— Provided by publisher.
 Audience: K to grade 3.
 Includes index.
 ISBN 978-1-63470-721-3 (hardcover) — ISBN 978-1-63470-751-0 (pbk.) — ISBN 978-1-63470-736-7 (pdf) — ISBN 978-1-63470-766-4 (ebook)
 1. Butterflies—Juvenile literature. 2. Children's questions and answers. I. Title.
 QL544.2.M18 2016
 595.78'9—dc23
 2015026084

Cherry Lake Publishing would like to acknowledge the work of The Partnership for 21st Century Skills.
Please visit *www.p21.org* for more information.

Printed in the United States of America
Corporate Graphics

Table of Contents

My big eyes see colors you can't see.

My curly tongue works like a drinking straw.

I come
in many
colors and
patterns.

I fly very well on my thin wings.

I love to visit flowers.

I taste with my feet!

15

When I am young, I eat and eat.

Then I turn into a **pupa** for a while.

Do you know what I am?

I'm a Butterfly!

About Butterflies

1. Most butterflies feed on the **nectar** of flowers.

2. The butterfly's wings are made up of tiny, colorful **scales**.

3. A butterfly has four stages of life. They are the egg, caterpillar, pupa, and butterfly stages.

4. Some butterflies **migrate**. That means they fly very long distances.

5. There may be more than 20,000 different kinds of butterflies.

Glossary

migrate (MYE-grate) to move from one area to another

nectar (NEK-tur) a sweet liquid in flowers

patterns (PAT-urnz) a group of colors, shapes, and figures that are repeated

pupa (PYOO-puh) the stage during which the animal has a hard case to protect itself

scales (SKAYLZ) small, thin, flat body parts that overlap one another

Index